House of Sighs

House of Sighs

A Novel by Jocelyne Saucier

Translated by Liedewy Hawke

THE MERCURY PRESS

The publisher gratefully acknowledges the financial assistance of the Canada Council for the Arts, the Ontario Arts Council, and the Ontario Tax Credit Program. The publisher further acknowledges the financial support of the Government of Canada through the Book Publishing Industry Development Program (BPIDP) for our publishing activities.

Edited by Beverley Daurio
Composition and page design by Beverley Daurio
Printed and bound in Canada
Printed on acid-free paper

1 2 3 4 5   05 04 03 02 01

Canadian Cataloguing in Publication Data

Saucier, Jocelyne, 1948–
House of sighs : a novel
Translation of: La vie comme une image
ISBN 1-55128-091-4
I. Title II. Series
PS8587.A38633V5313 2001   C843'.54   C2001-903001-0
PQ3919.2.S23V5313 2001

The Mercury Press
BOX 672, STATION P, TORONTO, ONTARIO CANADA M5S 2Y4
www.themercurypress.ca

House of Sighs

A Novel by Jocelyne Saucier

Translated by Liedewy Hawke

THE MERCURY PRESS

The publisher gratefully acknowledges the financial assistance of the Canada
Council for the Arts, the Ontario Arts Council, and the Ontario Tax Credit
Program. The publisher further acknowledges the financial support of the
Government of Canada through the Book Publishing Industry Development
Program (BPIDP) for our publishing activities.

Edited by Beverley Daurio
Composition and page design by Beverley Daurio
Printed and bound in Canada
Printed on acid-free paper

1 2 3 4 5   05 04 03 02 01

Canadian Cataloguing in Publication Data

Saucier, Jocelyne, 1948–
House of sighs : a novel
Translation of: La vie comme une image
ISBN 1-55128-091-4
I. Title II. Series
PS8587.A38633V5313 2001   C843'.54   C2001-903001-0
PQ3919.2.S23V5313 2001

The Mercury Press
BOX 672, STATION P, TORONTO, ONTARIO CANADA M5S 2Y4
www.themercurypress.ca

To Dondie,
my sister, my friend

Whenever I stir up my childhood memories, a smell of menstruation begins to drift over them. This has never amazed me, although it seems unlikely that any body odours could have resisted my mother's vigorous washings. She was fanatical about cleanliness, and if certain smells did manage to escape her vigilance, they could only be those of disinfectants, deodorizers, and other chemicals connected with the relentless war she waged against all household parasites.

Even so, since that time when as a little girl barely four years old I pushed open the bathroom door which was slightly ajar and saw her remove that red thing from the bottom of her panties, the smell of menstruation has always stuck with me.

I knew she was menstruating that day. She had told my father so at lunchtime. "I am having my period," she had said to him. As young as I was, I knew what those words meant (she was losing the blood of the baby who didn't want to be born, she had explained to me). Actually, I think that after the flowers one mustn't touch, after the horrible puréed spinach that makes little children grow, and after the pooh in the potty, the bleeding that was visited upon my mother every month was one of the first realities of the world given to me to discover.

She was about to menstruate, she was menstruating, or she had just menstruated: our family life revolved around my mother's periods.

My father and I were continuously waiting for what she had to tell us about her menstrual cycle. That usually happened at mealtime. This is how, between the soup and the dessert, we heard about the circumstances under which ovulation had taken place, the condition of the mucus, the disturbances occurring in her womb and, when the cycle reached its peak, the course her menses were following, with the necessary details about the colour, consistency, smell, and the heaviness of the bleeding. All these things mattered greatly to our little family because, from one twenty-eight-day span to the next, we were living to the rhythm of the changes experienced by my mother's body.

My father was touchingly patient. He always listened to her without ever interrupting unless he felt she would like him to, in which case he commented on the situation or asked a question, showing the exact degree of anxiety or relief that was needed.

Sitting very quietly at my end of the table, I understood much of what was being said. I occasionally asked questions, although these weren't always as appropriate as the ones my father posed.

"What's your mucus like today, Mama?" She would be moved by my concern and take the time to explain.

"The mucus, my little darling, was three days back, two beddy-byes ago. It had egg white in it as big as a chickpea. There's no more mucus now. Discharge has taken the place of the mucus. And it's because of the discharge that Mama has to wear pads to protect her undies."

So we had a menstrual cycle, regular and fateful, of twenty-eight days controlling our family life down to the smallest detail. Our diet (salads *before*, liver *during*, and sugar *after*) would vary according to the demands imposed by hormonal imbalance. Our activities did, too. Inviting little girlfriends over when my mother had her period was totally out of the question, as was the idea of my father agreeing to work overtime for his employer. My mother spent the week of her menstruation lying on the sofa in the living room, pale and languid under three thick woollen blankets and yet always shivering. We had to protect her from the jolts of everyday existence during this week, when the zest for life leaked out from my mother at the same time as her blood.

Before he left for work, my father had done all the

essential household chores, settled my mother on her sofa, placed indispensable articles around her so that she only needed to reach out a bloodless hand from beneath her woollen blanket in order to pick up a glass of water, a tablet or — if she still had the strength and the determination — a book. And when I got back from school, I would sit down by her side on my tiny chair and wait for that moment of pure happiness when she would open her eyes and slowly, gently, stretch her dry white lips into a thin smile and ask me drowsily, "Now then, my little darling, tell me, what have you done today?"

I loved that image of my mother, fragile and wistful like a beautiful fairy-tale princess. I adored the meditative atmosphere there was in the house then. And I dreamed of the time when I would carry within me the mystery belonging to women.

I think she shared my dream, because the day she discovered my red-stained panties in the laundry she greeted me when I got home from school with a triumphant, conspiratorial air. The sofa and the whole menstruation kit were waiting for me in the living room.

I wasn't twelve years old yet when I made my way into the esoteric secrets of the female world, where my mother, I'm sure, had been expecting me since the moment she learned she had just given birth to a little girl.

We now had two menstrual cycles whose course we needed to follow with meticulous attention. Not a single meal went by without us having cause to exchange some news about our respective organs. My mother, whose menstrual periods were actually much more exhausting than mine, fretted constantly: "What's your mucus like today, my little darling?"

And now that I knew the consequences of ovulation involving the right ovary (heavy menstruation) or the left one (very painful menstruation), now that I could interpret my vaginal mucus and discharge, I took great care to give precise and detailed answers to these questions.

"I only had a thin trickle of mucus this morning. It was like what I had last month, but different, because it was thicker and completely clear."

The menstruation ceremonial, then, took place twice a month and reached a pitch of fervour as yet unequalled when our menstrual periods came to intersect, then to overlap and, finally, to merge entirely, so that my father had to put a camp bed in the living room. I remember his look of alarm the first morning he saw us both settled down there for a week of camping.

From that moment, the house took on the appearance of a place of worship, a monastic mood which clung to it long after I had gone off to live somewhere else and my mother had entered menopause. Even to this day, when I visit her and happen to find the living-room curtains drawn, the three woollen blankets on the sofa, and my mother gently floating in that muffled atmosphere, I have the feeling that time didn't really stand still and that my father is going to materialize from the photograph on the wall and sit down in the armchair beside which his pipe and slippers still wait for him.

I think it was the year my mother and I took to camping in the living room that my father left us.

Although we had a happy life, I used to believe I was destined for unhappiness.

I had an example, an idol — Aunt Clara, the eldest of my mother's sisters, the only one I knew, actually. The others, and there were quite a few of them, would only turn up accidentally in my mother's conversation; not once were they invited over to our house, nor have we ever gone over to theirs.

Aunt Clara had known all the misfortunes that set a life apart: a violent husband, three stillborn children, a hysterectomy, breast cancer, the seizure of all her furniture, ungrateful children, noisy neighbours, and goodness knows how many nervous breakdowns. There had also been — but that was very distant and very secret — repeated rapes at the beginning of her teenage years. "I was branded." That's how she put it to my mother when they would touch in veiled terms upon this exceptionally painful episode.

She was "my favourite aunt," as I liked to say to my little

school friends. And yet she didn't take any particular notice of me; she was hardly even aware I was there. But as soon as she thought I was old enough to appreciate the extent and the harshness of her misfortunes, I was accepted at the kitchen table where she would sit and talk about herself to my mother. I had been waiting for a long time to be admitted into the magic circle of Aunt Clara's confidential outpourings.

I remember. I had slipped into a chair at the table and, instead of smiling distractedly at me when my mother wanted to send me away, she said, "Let her stay, it's high time she found out what life's all about."

I was in seventh heaven! I was ten years old and still played with dolls, yet I was being welcomed as an equal by Aunt Clara, who had known all the tragedies that could possibly grace a person's life.

From as far back as I can remember, Aunt Clara was the heroine of my childhood games and daydreams. I swaddled my dolls like she did with her stillborn children, I gave them emergency baptisms, I sang them a song I didn't know the words to, a song as mournful as what I'd heard at our kitchen table, and after the funeral service, held in the shadowy light of my bedroom (curtains closed, chest of drawers converted into an altar and shoe box into a coffin) I went to bury them, but only symbolically of course, because another baby might die inside my aunt's body and I needed every one of my dolls so as to be prepared for all eventualities.

Sometimes, too, I became Aunt Clara as she lay dying of cancer, or was pinned to the stake by her dirty pig of a husband (I never heard her call him anything else), or facing a firing squad commanded by a bailiff. And depending on whether I was in a martyr-like mood or a heroic one, I would succumb with delight to each of these horrors or I would suddenly loom up in the middle of my daydreams as a shining, beautiful heroine, and I pursued, I provoked, I pulverized the hateful, vile, despicable individual who was tyrannizing my aunt.

Same thing with the books I read. Aunt Clara's image would slowly work its way into them, merging with that of Cinderella, Rapunzel and, later, when I pored over innumerable sentimental novels for young girls, with other great examples from the list of women martyrs. In those stories, the heroine was fragile, pure, delicate, and had to undergo an endless string of torments before finally realizing a noble destiny or dying a magnificent death. I could not possibly imagine a worthy life without these fantastic ordeals, and Aunt Clara's existence was not only richly adorned with them, it was also wonderfully recounted to us whenever she came to visit.

Her visits were unfortunately very rare, because she lived

in a town at the bottom of a valley that was swallowed up by snow or battered by rain and furious gales, so that she could only leave when there was a lull in the weather. I never went to see her in the days when she lived there. We had a car that could have taken us, but each time my mother talked about a visit to her sister, the car would mysteriously give out. I wouldn't be a bit surprised if I found out today that all the problems our car would suddenly be cursed with were a pure invention of my father — he didn't like Aunt Clara.

Heralded by a long letter and the weighed-down look my mother used to adopt after that, my aunt would arrive with her little cardboard suitcase and settle in for a few days.

She hadn't set one foot in the house yet when the bitter wind of adversity swept in.

It began, when the door had barely shut behind her, with the usual comments on the temperature, which even on a bright sunny day always somehow managed to be ominous.

"That sun's much too hot, it's going to scorch all the gardens."

And my mother would go one better: "If this keeps up, we're heading for a drought."

Then, one or the other would move on to a heat wave that had left people dead somewhere the year before, to the sunstroke that had confined a neighbour to her bed, and should the references to climatic devastation happen to run out, there was always an anonymous calamity reported on the radio or by the newspapers that gave them something to talk about while my aunt was being settled in my bedroom, my mother put the kettle on for coffee, and inexorably, imperceptibly, the conclusion would be reached to the leisurely progress of my mother and my aunt towards the kitchen table, where each would find her own chair, her own cup, and the previous visit's conversation.

"I tell you, it's no joke," one of them would begin. Usually my mother.

"No, it's no joke," the other agreed.

The remark didn't refer to anything in particular. It was simply a matter of getting in tune with each other.

A brief moment of silence, a few long sighs to get herself going, and Aunt Clara began to relate the melancholy news from her sombre valley. Aunt Clara was a good storyteller. She didn't neglect a single detail, didn't leave anything out that might be important to the rest of the story, and she knew how to linger over certain descriptions that were bound to capture my mother's full attention. And when she arrived at an especially painful point, she let a grave silence descend so we might appreciate the voluptuously acrid delight of that particular point in her story, and she'd only go on with her narrative after heaving a great, deep sigh which indicated that the worst was yet to come.

Now it was my mother's turn to sigh. The sighs and nods with which she punctuated my aunt's narration were the clearest proof that she caught every bitter drop of it. And if an exceptionally meaningful detail hadn't received the proper amount of consideration, she would wait for an emphatic sigh from my aunt to come back to it: "He took the money from the cookie jar?"

"He," pronounced in that tone of voice, was my uncle, of course, and the cookie jar testified to his appalling meanness.

"Yes, the cookie jar," my aunt repeated with another sigh. "It wasn't for the cookies. He never eats them, and he's the last person who'd ever hand out any to the children."

And to complete the picture of her husband's shameful behaviour, she explained the subterfuges he had employed in order to appropriate the money she'd been secretly saving up in the jar and which, instead of the dress that would have replaced the shapeless worn-out cotton thing she'd been wearing for years, had been used to buy two bottles of the very best liquor that could be found anywhere in their valley.

"After he sobered up, the first thing he did when he got back was pounce on the cookie jar. Naturally, he broke it."

On the day I was admitted into the circle of secrets at our kitchen table, "he" had brought a woman home to dinner.

"His mistress," my mother concluded as soon as that brazenly made-up woman turned up in my aunt's story.

Unfaithfulness was something new to be added to my uncle's disgraceful conduct. That is to say, I had never heard it mentioned until then. I only half realized just how awful an act this was. But I understood it well enough to envision that painted woman as a diabolical creature who was going to pound even more deeply into Aunt Clara's heart the stake my uncle had driven into it. This image delighted me while at the same time causing me intense pain.

I let out a long sigh of confusion. They promptly stopped talking. They'd forgotten all about me. They were just beginning to wonder whether that dirty pig of a husband might not infect the whole household with his painted-ladies diseases.

Impressed by the depth of my compassion, Aunt Clara stared at me for quite a while. Then she looked questioningly at my mother, who nodded her approval, and made this strange request to me:

"For a long time now I've been praying to the good Lord to take him back. He isn't listening to my prayers. Your mother is praying, too. But her prayers aren't listened to any more than mine are. It would be a blessing for everyone, though, if your uncle were to pass on. There's nothing wrong with asking for somebody's death if that somebody is the devil himself. Ask the good Lord for it in your prayers. That's perhaps what He is waiting for. The prayer of a pure soul, a young soul that hasn't suffered yet, that hasn't been tarnished by life. He doesn't pay attention to me any more."

I was so thrilled I could have shouted out with joy. But as young as I was, I knew this kind of happiness couldn't possibly be shared, and I quickly produced that knowing air I had observed in adults when they wanted to make it clear they had a firm grasp of the situation.

Not only was I allowed to sit at the table of sighs, I was being entrusted with a mission that was going to set Aunt Clara free from her life of suffering.

I prayed and I prayed. I prayed so much I didn't know what to dream up next to persuade God to take his horrible creature back.

Each time she returned for a visit, Aunt Clara inquired, "Are you still praying?"

I was still praying. With the terrifying hope that my prayer might be answered one day and thus might end the only real major tragedy I had been fortunate enough to witness at close range. My mother, my father and I led a happy, uneventful existence where everything was in its own cosy place, even the petty annoyances of daily life, and had it not been for the exhilarating wind carried into my routine by Aunt Clara's misfortunes, all I would have known was our domestic bliss, which was absolutely of no interest to the world of my imagination or to that of my girlfriends, who after each visit from Aunt Clara would be waiting for my detailed report.

I became the queen of my circle of friends. We would sit down together well away from the childish goings-on in the playground and tell each other about real life. On those lucky days following her visits, Aunt Clara and I occupied a full week's recesses. Afterwards, it took a while for our conversations to hitch solidly on to less convincing hardships: an authoritarian father, a tyrannical sister, household chores, and other little troubles my life was so miserably devoid of.

I would have found it difficult to convince my friends that my life wasn't a dull and dreary stretch of happy days. Whenever they came over, a delicious sweet smell wafted through the house, revealing what treat we were going to have that day, and my mother needed to show them the new dress she'd just made for me, or my bedroom my father had repainted, or some other little surprise thoughtful parents will have in store for a beloved daughter.

I acquired a friend, though, who took no notice of this great show of happiness. An only daughter like myself, she was much more pampered than I was, her father being the manager of a hardware store while mine was a simple postal worker. "They've got all kinds of money," sighed my mother

21

when she saw their furniture parade by on the day they moved into the house next door.

She was called Francine and was no older than me, but already acted the sophisticated lady. Her look of pity when she got to know our house opened my eyes to the abject poverty in which we lived. Instead of driving us apart, the gap in family wealth brought us together, with her telling me about the splendours of their life of luxury, and me, the miseries of our material troubles. She was a princess and I, a poor commoner.

We'd been having fun playing these roles for several weeks already when one night her mother came knocking on our door.

Aunt Clara had arrived in the afternoon. The conversation had become so intense that my bedtime was long past without my mother noticing. My father was in the living room. He had come in a short time ago, having exhausted all the outside activities that allowed him to avoid Aunt Clara's company. From the kitchen door, which faced the living-room door, I could only see the top of his balding head behind the pages of his newspaper.

It was my mother who went to answer the door.

In the hallway I heard the unsteady voice of our neighbour, who apologized for calling on us so late (my mother told her not to worry) and who said: "Now, I hope you won't take this the wrong way, dear. Francine has told us. This isn't much, but it may help..."

"What's?!..."

"Listen, there's no shame in needing help. And it's no hardship to us. Please, take it. We're glad to do it."

The front door closed again.

I then saw my mother struggling with a box overflowing with food, and so heavy she had to hold it at arm's length while she hesitated between the kitchen and the living room, unable to understand what was happening.

My father understood. And he blew up. "The neighbours consider us a charity case!" He flashed a black look at my mother, gave his newspaper an angry shake, and sank even deeper into his chair, which, with him, signalled an implacable fit of rage.

I went to bed without being told to. Aunt Clara joined me soon after. And until I managed to fall asleep, I could hear my father and mother muttering in the living room.

Aunt Clara's already infrequent visits now became extremely rare. Twice a year, at the most. At those times my father, a real stay-at-home, would suddenly discover he had a taste for bowling, for bridge, for the lively atmosphere of taverns, and would only turn up at the house very late at night, usually when everyone was asleep.

My friendship with Francine cooled off. Soon she became

just one of the several friends with whom I marvelled at the grand beauty of adversity and who would ask me occasionally, "Are you still praying?"

I was. With the same terrified hope.

One day the thing I hoped for and dreaded more than anything else in the world came true. My uncle died. Cirrhosis of the liver.

When my mother told me about it, there were so many confusing emotions inside of me battling with one another that I thought my heart would burst. My mother took me in her arms and I felt she was so strong, so mightily grown in stature due to the shock of the news, that I didn't need to think any more and could surrender to the comfort of tears.

She'd had time to look after everything. I was going to be consigned to our neighbours' care while she and my father went to the funeral, the luggage was ready, theirs as well as mine, they were leaving as soon as my father returned from the garage where he was having the car checked over for the trip, and they would be back in two days' time.

I worked it out and, through my tears, I realized we were going to be separated for three long days — an eternity.

The separation proved to be less excruciating than I had thought. I had so much to tell my friends during that interval that I forgot to count the hours and the days: my uncle's death, of course (I had to repeat the detailed description of it innumerable times), but also what my aunt had said to my mother when she announced the news to her over the telephone, and what my mother had said to me afterwards, and all the cruel things my uncle had done which they made me go over again and which convinced them that both his death and my prayers were justifiable, since in this way these words from the Bible were fulfilled: "He who lives by the sword, shall die by the sword."

If I had occasionally been troubled by scruples about invoking my uncle's death in my prayers, my girlfriends assured me that Aunt Clara would thank me for the rest of her life.

I almost believed myself to be in direct contact with God when, at the end of one recess, a girlfriend slipped in beside me in the lineup and asked, "Would you mind praying for me, too? If I fail the geography exam, I'll have to repeat my year."

And so the Earth didn't stop turning when my father came back without my mother. I was immune to all human failings. I had become a great dispenser of justice to the oppressed of this world.

She had stayed behind to help out. But that shouldn't keep her there for very long. "No more than a week," she promised in the letter she'd written to me, which my father gave me upon his return. It was the first real letter I received from my mother. Rapturously happy, I read all the recommendations and tender exhortations (the cod-liver oil capsules, the teeth, obedience to my father and my teacher) she presented me with, and only in the postscript did I find out what was happening: "Aunt Clara is in a state of shock. She needs rest. We are asking neighbours to take in your cousins for a while and I am bringing her back with me to our place."

The week dragged on in endless anticipation. I wore myself out picturing the look in Aunt Clara's eyes, her smile, what her voice would sound like when she saw me, the way she'd go about thanking me inconspicuously, without my father hearing.

On the eighth day of this eager expectation, I saw the suitcases in the hallway as I got back from school. I couldn't control my impatience and rushed into the kitchen without bothering to take off my coat and boots.

My mother greeted me with a stern look — I had left puddles on the floor — and my aunt, instead of welcoming me triumphantly, as I'd expected, with a face beaming with joy and gratitude, announced to me in a voice elated with grief: "What a tragedy, my poor child! What a tragedy! It's a great, great loss!"

I suddenly felt awfully small, much too small for life. It was then — I remember it as an inner ritual with me making a solemn promise to myself — that I made up my mind I was only going to watch people's unhappiness from inside my cosy existence.

I will still occasionally ask myself, before a bowlful of oatmeal or an avocado salad, if there are enough vitamins there to make me grow. And right away I will add some wheat germ to my oatmeal or watercress to my salad. At my age, one stopped growing a long time ago, but it is my job to look after the body my mother gave me and I must continue making it stronger. When I see people no older than me with dentures, liver trouble, digestive problems or, even worse, who are being treated by psychologists, I can't help thinking of their mothers. And imagining what was missing from their lives when they were children.

My mother saw to everything. And if I'm able to view the future with serenity today, it's thanks to her good care and attention. I am not afraid of sickness, or poverty, or any kind of mental distress; I was perfectly sure as a child of being fed, looked after, formed in body and mind so as to make me invulnerable to the miseries of adulthood.

I never questioned anything my parents suggested. They

devoted themselves entirely to my upbringing. Absolutely everything in the house and in our family life was conceived in relation to my well-being and the fine future that was being fashioned for me. This is why I had complete faith in all that was being planned for me and I never balked at anything. I would eat the horrible puréed spinach, swallow the concoctions my mother made up to strengthen my blood, stir up my neurons (before the end-of-year exams), and regulate my glands (during outbreaks of acne), I accepted the woollen camisole and the round-toed shoes even though my girlfriends had reached the bra stage and were wearing pointed shoes, I let myself be guided, moulded, steered by the skilful hands of my mother and all those who assisted her — my father, our family doctor, the dentist, the optometrist, my teachers — because I knew she was the best mother in the world.

My father was a wonderful support to her. He was the one responsible for my education where money was involved. Every Saturday, after our drive, we would sit down together at his small writing desk in the living room and keep track of my pocket money in a large red notebook. I was completely free to do what I wanted with my allowance, but I had to learn to keep an exact account of what were savings, necessary expenses, and trivialities. For example, the jujubes I was so fond of fitted into the category "Trivialities," but if I bought them somewhere three pennies cheaper by the dozen, those three pennies would join the column "Savings," and if I happened to share my jujubes with a less affluent friend, half of the expense would become useful because it taught me charity.

I still have those same three budget items in my day-to-day bookkeeping. My father's lessons have had some effect. A restaurant meal is a triviality but an unquestionably useful expense when it's to celebrate the birthday of a woman-friend from work, and it becomes a saving when I am the one who is being taken out. The figures never fluctuate wildly in my account books, the trivial has never gone rummaging around in the useful, nor the useful in my savings. "The only way to stay clear of chaos in one's life," my father would say. Chaos being wildly fluctuating figures, which led to debt, that horrible canker.

After the bookkeeping session I went back to my mother.

"Come, my little darling, we're going to see if you've grown."

Grown thanks to her meals, my nights of sleep, her care and attention, my youth — my mother would measure the good life given to me on the bathroom door. She had drawn a graph on it, with one-tenth-of-an-inch increases, that tracked my growth since I'd been old enough to stand up. The door was covered with her fine pen-drawn lines which were flecked with coloured dots in various places. Only a practised eye could see these and make out the red, blue, or yellow dotted lines they formed at the height of the head, the arms, the shoulders, whose upward movement they charted.

I loved that moment when shutting the bathroom door behind us we would enter the thrilling private domain of my body which was about to reveal its secrets to my mother. Because after the measuring against the graph on the door came the weighing, the herbal bath whose fragrant drifts of steam carried us into the blurry warmth of another world, then the inspection of my teeth, my ears, of every square inch of my body which surrendered to my mother's sweetly expert hands. Not even in the most sophisticated beauty institutes have I ever encountered subtle refinements like the ones I experienced in our bathroom.

So, back to the graph on the door. My mother checked to see if the past week had produced growth. And while she busied herself with taking my measurements, I delighted in the warm smell from her armpits, her great archangel wings opening and closing about me in the most exquisite way.

"That's good," she would say reassuringly as she put the coloured pencils back in their case.

It would always be good. Whether I had or hadn't added on a tenth of an inch at the roots of my hair, the tips of my fingers, at my crotch (we had to make sure my development was proceeding in harmonious proportions), the news was always good.

"There was no need to worry, you see? Your arms have just caught up with your legs. Now they have that tenth of an inch your legs gained two weeks ago."

How could I possibly have worried? I'd been totally unaware of that tenth of an inch missing from my arms. My mother only communicated her concerns to me when she no longer had any. Or when she'd found a solution. Which usually led us straight to a specialist. The dentist was the one we saw most often, because both my parents were burdened with dentures and she didn't want me to be struck down one day by the same disgrace.

The examination of my teeth was therefore the most delicate and most important part of her meticulous inspection. Equipped with a tiny flashlight and sometimes a magnifying glass when decay was attempting a sneak attack on the foundation of a molar, she scrutinized every tooth. And to make sure nothing escaped her, she would use a length of thick black sewing thread (we hadn't discovered dental floss yet) to dislodge fragments of food that might be concealing the yawning abyss of a cavity. This operation, in spite of but also owing to the zeal with which she went about it, sometimes made my gums hurt. I never let this show because I, too, feared the horrible spectre of dentures and because she was the very best mother in the world. I only needed to take a look at the others...

It's not that the mothers of my girlfriends were cruel, or promiscuous, but they were just a touch irresponsible. Actually, when I had girlfriends over to the house, my mother unfailingly tried to make up for their lackadaisical upbringing.

This constant concern of hers for the way children were brought up sometimes led to incidents. Like that time when I brought Bernadette home with me. A very pretty girl, with the kind of blond curls I would've liked to have, but fearful, shy, almost totally friendless. She had joined my class in the middle of the school year and this was the first time she had come over to our place.

"You poor little thing, doesn't your mother get you to do corrective exercises, then?" my mother asked her.

My friend's slight scowl changed into a look of wide-eyed amazement. She muttered some excuse to defend her mother's honour and tugged my sleeve so we'd go up to my room. She never came back to play with me.

It upset me that my mother's remark had frightened Bernadette away. I had taken her under my wing, and even though she was slightly cross-eyed, she would have been a very nice friend for me.

To comfort me my mother said, "It's not the squinting that's serious, but the character flaws it causes. It produces shy children with complexes who end up being deceitful and turn into liars — and who knows where all this might lead them?"

To suicide, I recently found out. I'd lost sight of her ages ago, as soon as she left school, in fact. Just as my mother had predicted, she'd become deceitful, turned into a liar, and in the end she'd felt so uncomfortable at school where she couldn't make any friends any more, that she'd dropped out before finishing her final year. I don't know what her life was like after that except that she had been married several times. I got the news from a colleague who lives with one of her ex-husbands.

My mother had an unusually keen intuitive sense about the future that was in store for "other people's children." I've had a chance to witness this on several occasions. One friend of mine, a hardworking, brilliant girl, the pride and joy of her parents and of her teachers who were continually holding her up to us as an example, wore herself out chasing after a reputation of being top of the class and settled into mediocrity with a man without a profession. My mother's verdict long before the fact: "Too much excitement. Not enough sleep." Another girl, whom I didn't know personally (she was older than I was) — we'd see her swish by our window, a pretty, slender little thing always closely followed by a troop of insolent young boys as she went hopping along like a frightened doe — one day hastily slipped out of town. "A baby before she's sixteen," my mother would say every time she saw her go past.

She had too much respect for the role to condemn those mothers who didn't do a good job with their children. She would never openly criticize, never lay any blame, never say, "In her place, I would've..." Her remarks had the chilling detachment of a medical report and were strictly intended for me. To get me to understand what I should or shouldn't do so that together we might make a success of my upbringing.

As for women who were childless, they were totally uninteresting. Such a woman might be dazzling because of her beauty or elegance, the cleanliness of her house or her occupation (this was rare at the time), but she lacked that essential quality that would have earned her our attention.

I don't have any children. It's an unsettled question between us although neither of us ever alludes to it. I would have needed a husband, a lover, a breeder, and the few men I've agreed to go to the movies with, I've never introduced to my mother.

She never warned me against men or marriage or sexuality or anything like that. As a matter of fact, she never talked to me about men at all. It's my girlfriends who initiated me into what was then called "the mysteries of life." Over at my place, in our bathroom. The summer I was ten.

It's still difficult for me to remember those conversations, the weird feelings they stirred up made me so terribly ill.

That summer had been particularly rainy and we'd been condemned to the same indoor games for almost all of the holidays. We'd go over to one or another's place, bringing along our dolls, skipping ropes, and exercise books. But with puberty approaching, it became harder and harder to confess we enjoyed these little-girl games, and there would always be someone in the late afternoon who would drag us off with her over to the bathroom mirror. As the summer wore on, we'd end up earlier and earlier at the mirror having fun with our hair, with makeup, and that delight of our teenage years: our bathroom conversations.

At my place, though, the conversation took a turn that threw my mind into confusion. Because at my place the bathroom was far away from the kitchen and very tiny — my girlfriends and I could only fit into it when the door was closed (it opened towards the inside) — we felt protected there from the world of grown-ups. And this is where those conversations about sexuality began — men, their desire for women, their genital equipment, since sexuality couldn't be taken to mean anything else in those days.

I can't remember just what was said the first time, but a

very sharp image remained with me of this male hand placed on the fly he couldn't close up again because he was pulling this unseemly thing out of it which Ghislaine, our friend, had actually seen when she went to get a notebook from the bedroom she shared with her older sister. The gesture made by this man, really only a boy barely out of adolescence, shocked us profoundly, yet also aroused our curiosity because of all that it concealed. We had a whole new world to discover. Each one of us had had a vague idea this world existed, but during that rainy summer it became fodder for our idleness, demanding to be explored. Which we did all summer, piecing together what each of us knew, or could guess, or imagined, what we could recall from the horrified gossip our mothers used to exchange, and what we managed to get out of the dictionary and the family encyclopaedia.

I went at it, too, with my comments and observations. Those first weeks of our holidays were taken up completely with the malicious pleasure of tracking down the adult world's most secret doings, and our conversations used to stay with me even in my innocently childish games.

One day that summer, however, I happened to see my father touching his pants, just as I must have seen him do hundreds of times before, to scratch himself or put his private parts back in place, and suddenly the image of that other man's hand on his fly came back to me. Then, and only then, did I start to think that my father was a man, too, that beneath his pants there was a lump of excited flesh which dishonoured my mother at least once a week (on Saturdays, according to what I'd just learned).

The rest of my summer was hopelessly spoiled. I couldn't get that image out of my mind. I would gag just looking at my father's hands, imagining where they went digging about on Saturday nights.

I finally decided I needed to talk to my mother, I needed her to reassure me — she wasn't really doing the thing that was referred to in our bathroom conversations, or at least she wasn't agreeing to it, was she?

The best time was Saturday night, when she and I were united in the most fundamental mother-and-daughter closeness and when afterwards, supposedly but improbably, she would be on her way to the bondage of the marriage bed. One cannot lie at such a time.

I chose to put the question to her during my herbal bath. "Mama, about babies..."

The terror in her eyes!

"Yes, my darling..."

A firm voice. She was quite determined not to show how alarmed she was. She dragged her sentence out, hoping, I guess, that I hadn't just asked THE question. But I'd started the ball rolling, I couldn't give up now. I summoned up my courage.

"Mama, for me to come into the world, did Papa do it, too?"

I think I heard her gulp.

"But my darling, it was love that brought you into the world. Only love. Your father and I wanted to have a little girl like you so badly. We put together all our love for you, for the child we wanted so much, a little girl with hazel eyes and hair as soft as silk, and when we held you in our arms for the very first time, we knew we would love you all of our lives, with all our heart, and with all our soul. It's because of the miracle of love that you came along, my darling, and you were just like we'd hoped you would be, with those little dimples in your cheeks when you smile. Come on, my darling, let's see that lovely smile of yours, show me your dimples."

She talked to me a lot about love that evening. I almost felt reassured.

When Monday arrived and my girlfriends and I met up in our bathroom again, I tried to dissociate my family from all that had been said there over the past weeks. I blurted out, "For me it's different, my birth came about through love, nothing but love."

I remember. I was sitting on the toilet seat, staring down

at the floor with my legs casually swinging one on each side of the toilet bowl.

"So it was like the Blessed Virgin?"

They tittered in that shrill, snickering way little girls do when they decide to pillory one of their own. I didn't protest but I held on to the idea.

I didn't talk to them again about the miracle of love I had sprung from, they would have excluded me from those conversations I didn't want to miss in spite of everything, but I clung to the improbable hope that the laws of conception were not universally applicable and my parents had been exempted from them.

I held on tight to that notion of my mother's immaculate conception, even though doubt continually lurked somewhere in my mind. And if I still occasionally gagged at the sight of my father's hands, I would immediately dive into my chest of dreams to convince myself of his innocence.

I would've held out if my girlfriends hadn't conspired to confuse me. During another one of those rainy afternoons, they asked me if my parents slept in the same bed.

"Well, you see, they're doing it."

Then they produced an article cut out of the newspaper and showed me this shocking, horrifying headline which I couldn't possibly ignore: "Twin beds spell the end of a couple's sex life."

At that moment doubt entrenched itself in my chest of dreams in the most disturbing way. It was leaking from all sides, the gaps needed to be closed but I didn't know where to turn for help. My father's hands made me feel sicker and sicker, I was losing my appetite (he always helped out with the meals), I was going to get thinner, my mother would be worried, we would have another discussion, all was lost if she had to confess to what really was too shameful to expose.

The inevitable happened. I lost weight, a lot of weight judging by my mother's anxious look. I also stopped growing — she didn't have a single tenth of an inch to tell me about, the graph on the door remained untouched. She wouldn't say anything although she sometimes let out a sigh, "You poor little thing..." which she instantly tried to make up for with a thin smile, "It's nothing, really." Our bathroom exchanges dwindled down to these melancholy notes.

We were both fading away. I grew thinner, weaker, and she became gloomier day by day. Long dark shadows appeared under her eyes and seemed to stretch out over her whole body.

One day, not a Saturday, she marched me off to the graph and measured me in such an authoritative way it scared me. Next, she jotted down some things in a notebook, compared these with the growth chart on the wall and announced, "Tomorrow we're going to see Dr. Marsan."

Our family doctor, a big fat gentleman who stank of digestive problems, was used to my mother's inappropriate visits. Normally he succeeded in calming her down with a lot of psychology and some prescription or other. This time, however, I don't know why, he stuck to psychology.

"Sometimes the growing process slows down before puberty. There's nothing to worry about. With time, things will sort themselves out."

My mother gave him a poisonous smile. Her faith in our doctor's competence had just taken a mighty blow.

She took me straight from Dr. Marsan's office to the presbytery. She wanted a miracle.

Our parish had its very own holy man. The asceticism of our little Father Perron (people said he and his housekeeper shared a single potato at dinner), his great piety, and the strange parables parishioners would pass around without understanding what they meant had given him an aura of saintliness. He was rumoured to be capable of performing miracles. The recovery of certain people couldn't possibly be explained in any other way.

The saintly man had a gift for seeing into people's minds. He asked my mother to leave us alone and knew right away what was going on.

"What is it that's bothering you, my child?"

I burst into tears. The searching gaze of our kind-hearted

priest freed me from all my inhibitions and I began to tell him how indignant I felt, how ashamed, and disgusted, and about that slim hope that my mother might be exempted from the degradation, and I begged him to explain the miracle of love to me, the real miracle of love, the one that had resulted in my birth and would save me from the loathing for my father's hands. I cried so hard I couldn't go on.

He drew a clean handkerchief out of his cassock for me and started to question me in his sweet, saintly voice. When he understood through my answers that I was bothered by my mother's immaculate conception, his expression took on a hint of sternness.

"You mustn't confuse things, my child. Mary's Immaculate Conception and Her Virginity are two great mysteries of our Mother Church. It was the will of God in His infinite wisdom that the Mother of His Son should be born without the stain of original sin. That is the mystery of the Immaculate Conception. It was also His will that She remain pure until the Assumption, up to the moment when She would join Her Son in Heaven. That is how She came to be touched by the grace of the Holy Ghost to become the Mother of God made flesh. Only one woman has become a mother through divine intervention and that is the Virgin Mary."

He set about explaining that the act between husband and

wife wasn't impure because it was willed by God, and that my mother hadn't lied to me, it really was an act of love that had brought me into the world, but I had to give up those unwholesome conversations with my little friends.

I almost felt reconciled with this sanctified version of the conjugal act. My sobs now only came in little gasps. Then he said something that totally shattered me.

"God has willed the conjugal act for the sake of procreation, only for the sake of procreation, so the Earth will be populated with His children."

I was panic-stricken. Complications at my birth had made my mother sterile, I knew this, she often talked to me about it to reassure me that I would never have to share her love with anyone else. So what was that double bed doing in their bedroom? I couldn't possibly ask our kind priest this question without revealing to him something I wouldn't even admit to myself.

I remember feeling the ground split open at my feet, and seeing darkness all around me. I bit my lip so I wouldn't scream.

The saintly man was out of his depth trying to cope with the silent hysteria of a little girl. He explained a few more things, but I couldn't understand them at all, then he blessed me and returned me to my mother, recommending she pray and give me "a little bit of baking soda with cream of tartar, in the morning on an empty stomach. Don't worry, she will get over it."

What happened next is still very painful to me. When memories take me back to that time in my life, I intensely experience the feeling I had then which poisoned my existence — my mother was deceiving me.

It was a horrible thought, but the evidence was right there. The double bed in their bedroom, the smell coming from it, and the noises I'd begun to listen out for — the double bed was without a doubt stealing my mother away from me once a week. Willingly, without reason or obligation, since she couldn't have children any more.

Not only had I lost my appetite completely, but I came to actually loathe food. I would bring up everything I swallowed. Those few terror-filled days when the house was turned upside down have left me with this one distinct memory: I am leaning over the toilet bowl, crying and moaning with pain, waiting for yet another wave of vomit but it won't come, my mother who is standing behind me is trying not to show her panic, "Relax, my darling, don't force it, it's over," she freshens up my face with a cool moist towel while I wait, I desperately wait to hear her ask what the priest had asked: "What is it that's bothering you, my child?"

She really did ask me that question. And this is where my memories all blend into one, where my vision of the past slips away. I simply can't remember what I answered her, what we said to each other — nothing, a blank, faded, bleached-out conversation. My memory suddenly races along, short-circuits time, refuses to give me an accurate account of the events that followed, and it only offers me a dependable recollection, a true image, from the moment when I saw two men shove my parents' double bed into a truck and carry a set of twin beds up to their bedroom.

My father had already been gone for three years when I found out he had left us. I admire my mother's courage, I admire her moral strength and all that it must have taken in the way of guts and ingenuity for her to continue running the house and keeping my father's presence alive as though she really believed what she was telling me, that he'd been transferred to another position and then another one, in another town, always further away, there was nothing we could do about it, a man's work sometimes demanded sacrifices from his family. I wonder how long she would have held out if I hadn't told her one day that I knew.

My parents always had a harmonious relationship. I had no reason at all to be alarmed as she announced to me, when I got home from school, that he'd been sent to the North to replace an employee who'd been in a serious car accident. "You know what Papa is like, always ready to help out. Besides, it's a promotion, he's going to be assistant postmaster up there." He'd be away three months, since one of the poor man's lungs had been perforated by a rib.

They must have agreed on the way he was going to leave so as to spare me the distress of having to say goodbye. Yet I am still convinced that even if my father had been mulling over his decision for a long period of time (perhaps for several years, he was a cautious man), he didn't tell my mother about it until shortly before he left, otherwise they would have taken months to prepare me for it.

I was never aware of the pain she may have felt. She quietly carried on with her task of bringing me up. Under no circumstances did unhappiness ever disturb our daily routine. There were certainly moments of anguish, moments that should have worried me — a sudden hoarseness to her voice, her gaze clouding over and then hardening, a bad-tempered gesture, a sigh, a hint of sadness — my mother's grief must have surfaced once in a while, but our everyday life was humming along so reassuringly that I never noticed anything.

They must have agreed as well (or she had insisted on it) on the money orders he was going to send us every month together with a letter in which he assured me he loved me very much, was thinking of me, and felt intensely miserable about being so far away from me. Not a word, however, about him coming home, it was up to my mother to keep that illusion going.

Whenever she needed to tell me my father's homecoming was delayed, she came up with a suitable explanation. First there was that poor man (I never found out his name) whose health deteriorated to the point of being beyond recovery: an infection caused the perforated lung to become gangrenous, then it spread to the stomach, the spleen, they also began to fear for the liver, the colon, the small intestine. Each endangered organ would keep my father away a little longer. My mother and I followed the progression of the disease in a full-colour illustration in the *Larousse Encyclopaedia*. Each new centre of infection was an excuse for an anatomy lesson: "The spleen, you see, is right behind the stomach. It's an organ that's very important for the blood, it plays a role in the formation of red corpuscles." The *Larousse* illustration, already an unappetizing sight with its oozing red colours, took on a pus-like green hue in my mind as the infection spread further and further. I felt very sorry about all the mishaps suffered by the poor man's organs, so much so that I sometimes forgot to be upset about my father.

There came a time when it would have been necessary to invent some new organs for that poor man, and this is when despicable public-service intrigues began to prevent my father from coming back to us and taking up his old job again. My mother went to enormous lengths to make it clear to me how complex and petty these manoeuvres really were. With the help of an organization chart of the Post Office which she had found in a drawer of the writing-desk in our living room, she made me follow, box by box, the slow progress of an insignificant little clerk who was forcing out, in a straight line or diagonally, other employees occupying boxes above him, to finally pull himself up to the one my father filled.

My father had already been gone for nearly a year when she produced the organization chart from the desk drawer. By then the infection had reached the duodenum and the clerk had advanced by three boxes.

The name of the schemer, Paul Tallerant, was crossed out with a soft lead pencil in the box where he'd started from and copied out three boxes higher up. All the various comings and goings of personnel which the ambitions of that Tallerant had caused showed up in the erasures and arrows she had added to the chart. My father was still valiantly holding on to his place, but the red-ink mark circling his box indicated how precarious that position was. I grasped this without needing any further explanations.

"If Papa doesn't come back right away, that man is going to steal his job."

That "right away" must have alarmed her.

"Not so fast, my little darling, we aren't quite there yet. There are five more boxes to go before he reaches Papa. It takes a little longer than that."

She needed to draw things out, since my father wasn't supposed to lose his position until a year later. By the time a miracle treatment had made each of our poor man's organs healthy again, first the small intestine, then the colon, then all his other damaged vital parts got back their bright *Larousse* colours and the dear man was able to return to his job, but not my father, because his old position now rightfully belonged to the schemer.

That second year was very busy, since we needed to track the climb of the little clerk and the regeneration of those organs, the organization chart and the *Larousse*, without having any time off really, for if the clerk's professional ascent occasionally stood still, the miracle treatment would immediately bring about some spectacular fresh development in our patient's state of health. Not a week went by without my mother coming with some news that could change our lives. I never inquired where she got her information. She needed only to tell me this or that and I would believe her and right away go and get a clear picture of the new information in the *Larousse* or the organization chart, both left within arm's reach on the coffee table — an exceptional breach of our house rule which didn't allow anything to be moved out of place.

There came a day when she had to tell me that my father had lost his job. She couldn't delay indefinitely either the patient's recovery or the realization of the schemer's ambitions. My father was bound to end up unemployed and my mother embarked on another course to justify his absence.

She had chosen a Saturday, a day off, which gave us a whole day to ourselves and allowed her to break the news to me very slowly, "Did I tell you that our patient is completely well again?" She watched me more and more intently as the gloom of dusk settled over us and the moment drew near when night would fall on the inescapable catastrophe. "That Tallerant, you know, finally got what he was after."

Since he went away, my father had almost become an abstract figure, a symbolic character with whom I fed my imagination, the better to admire my mother's extraordinary courage. It wasn't so much his return any more that preoccupied me, but the necessity to support my mother in her efforts to give me the kind of happy family life she was trying so desperately to create. So when she finally told me this news she had been picking at since morning, it was more to reassure her than to make myself feel better that I said, "Well, then, if he hasn't got a job any more, he must be coming back!"

I caught her unawares, I think, because she suddenly looked annoyed. But my mother's amazing ingenuity wasn't at the end of its resources.

"Better than that! He's had a promotion. He's been made postmaster in a village thirty miles further north."

This is how from that Saturday on, instead of despairing

of a homecoming that was continually in suspense, we started to follow my father's career in those little northern towns where he collected promotion after promotion, a career that would bring him back to us, she assured me, as "postmaster, right here, in our own town, can you imagine that!" And to celebrate the glory of those promotions and his triumphant return, we went out to eat at a restaurant.

I don't know what else she would have invented. The promotions were doomed, however, to stand in the way of a gloriously triumphant return. I am sure she would have thought of something. I can just see her studying the map of the North while I was away at school, choosing some town where my father's career would have been tripped up by a far more ambitious colleague; I can easily picture her sitting there masterminding some convoluted scheme, and then announcing to me when I got back — that's how she always went about it — that we needed to be patient yet again, since my father's wandering had just launched him on a whole new adventure.

In spite of occasional Don Quixote-like episodes, which weren't at all in keeping with my father's character (he was more the Sancho Panza type and even less heroic than that), I never doubted my mother. Her explanations always fitted together perfectly and left no room for anything that could possibly have shaken the conviction that I had a happy family life similar in every respect to the one I used to know. Admittedly, my father was absent, but this was strictly temporary.

My girlfriends weren't quite so easily satisfied: "What! He won't even be home for Christmas?"

The first Christmas without my father was, I agree, not very believable. A few weeks before, my mother had paved the way for a tremendous snowstorm that would block the roads and prevent my father from travelling. "We're going to say a novena at Sacré-Coeur so that nothing will stop Papa from being with us at Christmas. You never know with those north winds, they can suddenly change into a freak storm..." The novena turned out to be powerless against the snowstorm and my girlfriends.

"Isn't there an airport up there?"

"It's closed, too, because of the blizzard," explained my mother, whom I had gone to ask.

"But how about after the blizzard has stopped?"

"Then he goes back to work, the Christmas holidays will be over." I didn't need to go to my mother, I knew the answer, she had been asked that same question a few days earlier by one of her women friends — I only needed to repeat what I'd heard.

Our female friends were making life rather difficult for us. I don't doubt for a moment that their questioning was prompted by the kind part of the human heart, the part that loves its neighbour, feels for him and wishes him well. At least, during the first year. After that, it seems to me we were faced with a cross-examination. They came with more specific, slyer queries. Sometimes my mother took offence.

Fielding their questions became almost more important than tracking my father's odyssey. Besides, the interest our situation aroused widened our circle of friends. My mother now suddenly had to entertain women who didn't even live in our area but were brought along by a friend or a neighbour and who, while pretending to feel sorry for us, inquired about "the latest news from the North" with questions so baroque that you wondered if they really expected an answer. I always listened very carefully to what was being said around our kitchen table. I knew that sooner or later, either at school or a friend's place, or a friend of a friend's place or at home (more than anything else I dreaded the bathroom conversations where diplomacy tended to be brushed aside), I would have to deal with those same questions. It seemed as though, within a ten-block radius, the female population of all ages wanted to know what was going on.

I became very good at this game. As time went by, I even turned less and less to my mother for answers and actually dreamt up a few of my own. Once, I caught her giving one of my fabrications in reply to a lady who was pouring out a stream of consoling platitudes in our kitchen. It didn't bother me in the least — I had developed such zeal in the battle my mother and I were waging against our hostile world, that I valued this new proof of our indestructible solidarity all the more.

We were never as close to each other as we were during those three years. At first, I let her protect me. Then, as people's interest in us grew more and more intrusive, I felt our happiness would be undermined from within if we didn't have strong walls to defend it. I was thirteen or fourteen at this time, my mother hadn't noticed I had become a teenager, yet she accepted me as a partner, almost her equal, though she still called me her little darling, and together we went over the points that were especially difficult to explain, we tested several different ways of getting around these — we were spending our days in a world of pure make-believe.

I remember. The second Christmas. How we managed to solve the problem.

We had just received our November money order. Sometimes the money order came with a letter for my mother. I have never known what those letters actually said, because she withdrew to her bedroom at those times and wouldn't come out again to give me a report until much later. I always enjoyed those occasions, since they introduced something new into our lives, my own letters from my father telling me nothing more than he loved me, was devoted to me, and felt very badly about being separated from me — all this in words that hardly varied from one letter to the next.

Christmas was approaching, we'd already begun to think of the decorations, my mother's letter would surely give us some indication of what to expect.

The news wasn't too awful, he had the flu. "A bad case of the flu," she took care to emphasize.

"Let's just hope there won't be any complications," she added.

"Well, in that case he'd definitely come home. He'll get much better treatment in our hospital than at his local clinic."

"Yes, you're right, he would be coming home then."

I very much wanted my father to be with us at Christmas and I felt certain my mother wanted it just as much. But from the way she folded up the letter with a sigh and especially from her furrowed brow, I could tell he wasn't going to come and that I had to help her to break the news to me.

"What else does he say in his letter?"

"Not a lot... oh, but wait a minute, that clinic you just mentioned... well, there have been two cases of meningitis."

"Meningitis... is that dangerous? Could Papa get it?"

"More than anything else, it's extremely contagious. Yes,

he could catch it. If he does, our hospital wouldn't accept him, no hospital would. He'd be treated up there, in the clinic, so the epidemic wouldn't spread."

"Is it dangerous? Could he die from it?"

The possibility that my father might die was much too disturbing to consider and not really practical, for how would my mother afterwards account for the money orders which was all we had to live on? I hadn't thought of the money orders, it was my mother who brought it up: "How would we manage? We've never been able to afford life insurance."

Yet the idea of my father's death stayed with us all evening. To think he might die was very uncomfortable. I felt vaguely guilty. That night, I remember, I had a horrible nightmare where I saw him sinking into a river that was as thin as a line on a map and then it got wider and wider until it sucked me into its oceanic depths which closed over my head and opened up again with a loud burst of laughter. The dream faded away, but left me in a drowsy state in which I still searched for my father and he came to get me and took me back to those slabs of water that kept on colliding and swallowing each other up, emerging suddenly and sliding away again behind enormous waterspouts in which loomed the slimy, wailing mask of my father who pursued me relentlessly all night long. I woke up convinced the meningitis epidemic would spare him.

My mother had spent a much more productive night. When I came down to the kitchen, she called me over to the window so we could marvel together at the beautiful weather. And while we prepared our breakfast she hummed an old Christmas tune, trying very hard to teach me its refrain.

"It's so silly of me, you know," she began in a breezy tone of voice when we were eating, "I completely forgot Papa already had meningitis when he was a small child. It wasn't until I thought about all this again last night in my bed that I remembered. He told me about it a long time ago. He almost died, they had even sent for the priest."

"Is it like the mumps? He can't get it a second time?"

"No, he can't. He's immune to it now. But I'm very much afraid he won't be able to come at Christmas. The village is sure to be quarantined because of the epidemic."

There was no longer any doubt in our minds about the epidemic. We therefore told our friends about these two cases of meningitis. Little by little the epidemic spread to my father's village and to our neighbourhood, which without being overly surprised went along with our spending the holidays on our own.

The third Christmas posed no problem whatsoever. I think by then our friends were simply leaving us to our illusions. There were no questions asked. Nevertheless, my mother and I had to come up with an explanation that would keep our camouflage intact. We were so totally caught up in our fantasies that I cannot even remember what the invention was.

I must admit that because of their lack of questions, their silence, their obvious indifference to the absurdity of our situation, my girlfriends had cracked the delicate foundations on which our happiness was built. I was quite ready to accept as true the revelation awaiting me one afternoon in a bathroom get-together.

Actually, nobody told me anything. That was the whole tragedy.

We were at my place, in our bathroom, and we were talking about boys. My friends were very well-behaved girls, but there would always be someone slipping into our group who was saucier than the others and came to cause trouble and disturb us, until we made it clear to her that we weren't having any of that. Some adapted themselves to our group and stayed on. Most of them, though, would flit about for a little while longer and then end up where they really belonged, at the chips stall, with the gang who hung around with the riffraff there and kept the local gossip mill going.

Just such a girl, I don't know who'd brought her along, had been annoying us all afternoon with her stories about boys she wanted to go out with, or wouldn't go out with any more, or not yet, or never again. All afternoon we'd had to listen to her squawking, because she was so wound up she didn't talk, she shrieked. After she left, we all agreed the girl was a lost cause.

Nicole, the most sensible one in our group, kindly spoke up on her behalf: "You've got to understand, her parents are about to split up."

They stole a quick look at me.

"What! But that's terrible!"

I was absolutely stunned. In those days and in our circle, a marriage break-up was an evil that only happened to degenerates. Artists, people in high places, their love affairs, their scandalous lives — this curse was something you only read about in the newspapers. That it might affect somebody we actually knew was completely inconceivable.

My girlfriends, very intent on not saying anything more, let me panic at the news.

"But don't you realize? It's awful! Her parents are breaking up! What's going to become of her now?"

Total silence.

They exchanged glances, nudged each other discreetly. I knew what that meant, a conspiracy of silence, a secret I wasn't let in on.

I just couldn't understand it. Here I was the most faithful, the most loyal member of the group, and yet they were hiding something from me. It was very aggravating, extremely humiliating.

I looked at each of them. I wanted to shatter the silence, force one of them to break rank and explain what was happening. Only Nicole would look me in the eye. Long enough for something to come apart.

"What's the matter with all of you? This is getting to be really annoying. You're keeping something from me, while I always tell you everything. You knew her parents were separating but you didn't tell me about it. I'm sure there's something more. Why are you all being so secretive? There shouldn't be any secrets between friends. I've never kept anything from you. When my father..."

Suddenly, an icy silence.

There was an impulse to reach out to me. They all wanted to come to me, help me, comfort me. The gesture remained unfinished, trapped inside their hearts, and revealed to me better than anything else what it was they could have told me.

There are certain moments when you would like to step outside of your life, and while you aren't in it, erase the memory of the recent past. I wish this moment had never taken place.

There must have been something absolutely terrifying about me. They didn't dare come near me. The revelation I

had just received destroyed three years of illusions and expectation. I was utterly crushed. Not so much because I felt sure
I would never see my father again, or because he had
abandoned us, or because of the impropriety of our situation
— I couldn't blame a person who after a three-year absence
no longer even seemed real. What upset me so terribly was
the realization that my mother was innocently cooking supper
(I could hear the rattling of the pots and pans) and that she
would have to go from a state of blissful ignorance to the
torture of the tongs that were digging about in my insides in
search of any sliver of flesh still holding out against the truth.
The caustic burn of the truth is the most agonizing thing there
is, and while I was completely consumed by it I saw my
girlfriends, horrified by my reaction, break away from the
group one by one and quietly slip out of the bathroom.

Afterwards, they never asked me any questions about it.
They knew and I knew where the matter stood. The subject
was closed, no longer relevant. And if it happened to turn up
by chance in some conversation, we always found a way to
skirt around it. They were true friends. Even today, among
those I am still friends with, not one ever tries to find out what
has become of my father and his money orders, or whether I
would like to see him again.

The same thing goes for my mother. After I told her, she
never talked to me about my father again. We carried on with

our lives as though we had always lived like this, severed from a person who didn't exist and whose absence was obscured by our concern never to say anything about it. The money orders kept arriving regularly, on the fifteenth of each month. We received no more letters, though. Those money orders, those cheques I sometimes wondered about, allowed us to live without any financial worries; they made it possible for my mother to have her asthma looked after and for me to go to university.

We kept his photograph on the living-room wall. So that I remembered him as he was on that photo, with a lot more hair than he had when he left and that half-smile aimed at the photographer. I sometimes caught my mother returning his smile. She could stand in front of that photo for a long time, motionless, vaguely smiling, as before an icon, wrapped up in thoughts that would slowly grow leaden with bitterness, for her smile would collapse and she'd arm herself with indifference and dismiss those thoughts with a determined sigh. If she spotted me at such a moment, she would drive me away with one of those black looks I had got to know so well.

In a certain sense, our lives were much more peaceful now. We didn't need to convince ourselves of anything any more, or defend indefensible fantasies for the benefit of the women in our circle. I suppose the word had got around.

They knew that we knew, and vice versa. There were no more cross-examinations in our kitchen.

Our lives continued in a normal way. I was a teenager, then a young woman, I got my degree, a profession, an apartment. We have watched each other growing older. The body's weaknesses have a twenty-year time lag with me, but I like to detect them in my mother, I like it when she says to me, "Now *that*'s the beginning of a varicose vein, but if you keep your legs elevated for five minutes every morning, you won't get them." I like to think we are the same age or will be some day. Only during these moments of worship of both our bodies does a slight thrill of pleasure at being alive come back to her. Only at these times is there no chance of my catching that sombre look she still sometimes has, a very pale residue of that black look she flashed at me when I finally told her.

I simply couldn't have done anything else. I had to tell her.

I couldn't let her go on living in a dream world while I was in possession of the truth. That would have been disloyal and cruel, too, much crueller than the cruel truth that duty demanded I impose on her.

"Papa isn't coming back. He's left us."

We were eating. I wish I'd said it differently. I had

something better planned in my head, but she was terribly excited that evening about the dress she was making for me and wouldn't stop talking about it. While we were having our dessert, I felt this irrepressible surge of words forcing my lips open like something that needed to be said before the meal would end and my courage failed me.

The most horrible look came into her eyes. I will never forget it. It was as though the ground opened up in those eyes and the searing pain I saw there shouted at me, begged me not to look, not to go where her heart was slowly breaking. Then her look darkened, grew black with rage and seemed to scream at me: "How dare you?..." and then it was over, her expression went blank, she turned away from me and began clearing the table.

She never asked me when, where, or how I had found out and I never tried to explain it to her. There was a wide gap between us.

The months that followed were very difficult. My mother's black look hounded me, lay in wait for me where I least expected it, and there was this gulf lying between us which was getting deeper and wider all the time. As often as I could, I tried to bring us together again but, every time, I came up against that look of hers.

I have no idea what gave me the sudden flash of inspiration. I have no idea how, with one simple little phrase, I managed to brighten her look and persuade her to take me once again under her motherly wing.

The November money order had just arrived. The opened envelope sat on the kitchen table, and for a brief moment I thought it was just like before, that there was also a letter, an expectation, a happy prospect for us to explore, and I said automatically, "I don't think he'll be able to make it home for Christmas."

She smiled at me and agreed, "No, I don't think he'll be able to be here at Christmas."

If I enjoy living in the past so much, it is because my childhood was full of wonderful daydreams. Even the silliest ones still amuse me, and I like to go back to them, to start the dream from the beginning again, follow it along on its meandering course, invent a few new twists, linger over details that have always delighted me, such as those delicacies I would prepare for Robin Hood in that dream where I was his official assistant (I can't think of any other word for the part I assigned myself) — I've always remembered the exact recipe of those dishes and every one of the subterfuges I would employ to conceal the path that led up to the cave where I used to prepare them, Robin Hood being the only one who knew of my existence in Sherwood Forest. Sometimes, too, I was Maid Marian, but that dream wouldn't last very long, since Maid Marian was too high-born to suit me and too stupidly feminine, whereas I rode without a saddle, my bow and quiver on my back, my thick tresses hidden away under the green hat worn by Robin's band of merry men, galloping boldly off into the friendly forest. Robin couldn't really love anyone but me. His love was too chivalrous, though, to be expressed.

I fantasized so much, I exercised my imagination so exuberantly in my efforts to alter the books I read and the films I saw in order to cast myself in them, that I have trouble finding my bearings in what is served up today to people's imaginations.

I may sometimes agree to go to a film if it reawakens my old daydreams, but in spite of Technicolor and Dolby Stereo, the Robin I saw there again had a cardboard and stage-makeup feel about him; he was an insipid ninny who became ridiculous the moment he picked up a sword. No connection at all with my companion-at-arms with whom I lived through so many adventures and who, if it weren't for that code of honour between us, would lay a kind of love at my feet no woman in the world could receive without fainting from happiness.

Even now, I can still return to that magnificent forest, its smells, its cavernous depths, a sudden flash of sky in the thick foliage, and me, a beautiful damsel, a gentle and valiant warrior of the forest, I know all its paths and its dangers, I slip through it as effortlessly as a ray of sunlight and I can see, sense, and hear things that have escaped the vigilance of Sherwood's band of merry men, and this will save Robin from yet another ambush devised by the Sheriff of Nottingham.

I was just a little girl then and could only picture myself as a young woman in that fantasy. Still today, when I feel a sudden urge to go back to it, I become that lovely girl of the forest again. It makes me forget the arthritis that has started to eat into my bones.

Yet I don't think anyone ever regarded me as what could be called a dreamy child. For some reason daydreaming was associated with forbidden things and I always made sure no one caught me at it. To this day, when I am tempted to surrender myself to it again, even before I can feel myself drifting off, something is triggered in me, an extremely reliable instinct for camouflage, and I can tell that my mind is organizing itself to keep me alert, ready to respond to the call of reality and above all else to stop my eyes from staring vacantly into the distance, a sign of nonchalance which has always struck me as indecent.

I can mark my students' papers, take part in a meeting of the school board, talk with my colleagues, while I am totally engrossed in making a new life for myself in another world. It's a perilous exercise which requires continual watchfulness. I love being in that space between two universes. There is no greater freedom.

I haven't always had this skill. When I was very, very small, I needed to be completely sure that nobody, absolutely nobody, would catch me in the act. In my bedroom that was pretty easy. I would close the door, arrange my dolls on my bed, with a few of them on the chest of drawers or (I had exactly fourteen, one of them a negress) sitting primly at their little table facing my porcelain tea set; I would scatter the contents of my doll's house all over the room, especially in front of the door, so if my mother needed to come in to do housework or bring me some clean laundry, she had to manoeuvre delicately before she could slip in through the half-open door: "My darling, would you mind asking your little friends to move over a tiny bit?" The many-headed hydra I was pursuing with my sword had plenty of time to dissolve into reality.

What I liked more than anything else was my bedroom at night time. No more need to stage a performance for my mother, she thought I was asleep — I could conjure up all the lives I wanted. I ended up with chronic insomnia as a result of this game.

There were also our Saturday afternoon drives. My mother and father in the front seat and me in the back, my nose pressed against the window in case she happened to turn towards me to point out some cows or sheep on the horizon. I wouldn't have wanted her to see me staring blankly into space and say to me something like: "Well, now, have we drifted off into a daydream?" Those drives were our family outings for the week and were intended to show me what lay beyond the narrow confines of our little town.

And then there was the shed. I can still recall the smell of old oil and dust which I associated with my father for a long time. My mother hardly ever went there. It was my father's domain. He shut himself away in it almost every night for hours on end. I've never known just what he did there. Most of the time I was in bed when he came into the house. I would hear the doorknob turning and quickly curl up into a sleeping position because he occasionally came straight up to my room. I would concentrate so hard on my breathing so it wouldn't betray the fabulous world I had just emerged from that I felt as though I were actually sinking right into the mattress. He would open the door very gently, approach my bed, stand there watching me for quite a while, and then make up his mind to plant a little kiss on my forehead, whispering, "Goodnight, my little mouse." Or my little kitten, or my little bug, always the name of a small living creature. After that he would walk over to the window. Apart from the shed and some other rickety building in the alleyway, I really do wonder what it was that kept him gazing out my window for such a long time.

"Did you turn off the light in the shed?" my mother would ask when he went downstairs.

"I did. I just checked."

Yes, it had of a smell of old oil and dust, also of grass clippings (the lawn mower was kept in it) and scrap iron. I always went there in a roundabout way, I would never go straight from the house to the shed.

Sometimes the urge to daydream came over me when I was with my girlfriends. Usually it would be about Robin whom I had to set free from the Nottingham dungeon or from Maid Marian's simpering ways, or it would be about a strange scourge that I'd read about somewhere which had swept down on all the inhabitants of our town and demanded that one brave person offered himself up as a sacrifice, or about a war, a terrible predicament, or an immense sorrow, and I would feel as if my feet had wings. An exceptional destiny was waiting for me, which I didn't believe in of course, but which was a lot more fun than playing with dolls. So I would tell my friends I had promised my mother something, anything (lying didn't weigh heavily on my conscience) and I would dash to the shed through the alleyway. First I checked to see if my mother could see me from one of the windows, then I went to settle down in my own little corner between my father's workbench, the container of turpentine and his pile of old planks, and I would quietly savour my lovely fantasies.

Sometimes, too, but not as often, Robin showed up just

as my mother invaded my room with her rags, her disinfectants, her pail of sudsy water, or Aunt Clara would arrive with her little cardboard suitcase, or something else happened, and I needed to keep those restless fragments of daydreams waiting. It was impossible to go to the shed and tell my mother I was going to see my girlfriends — I would never have lied to my mother. It was also impossible to go there directly — she would've seen me and what would she have thought? So I took those bits and pieces of daydreams along with me over to my girlfriends' places and waited for an hour before slipping off to the alleyway.

The shed. I really liked it there. The smell, the light filtering through the thick layer of dust on the single window, the peaceful late-afternoon sounds in the alleyway, and even my father's clutter — me who can't stand untidiness — I loved all these things, I felt as if I'd left the world behind. Ensconced in my little corner which was just big enough to hold my bottom, with my back against the rough boards of the wall and my legs tucked up over the wood pile, I felt comfortable all the same. Wedged into that spot, I lived a splendid life radiant with wonder.

I never went back there after my father discovered me.

There had been a fire in the basement of the post office and he came to get his overalls so he could help clear away the debris. He sensed my presence right away.

"Well, well! There are all sorts of things going on in here," he said with a teasing smile when he saw me in my corner.

And as if he wanted me to know that he didn't mean to intrude on my privacy, he turned his back on me, rummaged around in the messy heap of his things while telling me all about the fire. I was mortified.

He took his overalls off the hook near the door, and still without a glance in my direction called out to me as he left, "There's nothing wrong with giving yourself pleasure, you know. Don't stay too long, though. Mama likes us to be on time for meals."

I thought then, and I still think, that he believed he'd caught me in the act of juvenile masturbation. It makes me blush just to think about it. I resented him for it.

From then on I began to practise conscious daydreaming. Even now, when I settle myself in bed with a daydream, I always keep in mind that my mother may phone me, that someone could come to the wrong apartment and knock on my door, that a fire or some catastrophe might bring a troop of first-aid workers to the foot of my bed and that I must be in a fit state to say and do what is expected of me.

When I really stop to think about it, it strikes me that fantasizing takes up almost all of my life. I can't imagine what my life would be like without the part devoted to daydreaming. I am not afraid of old age as long as I can revisit my childhood dreams.

Certain fantasies haven't lasted. They were too childish, too wild, too unreasonable. I still have a few images of them left, though, which I cherish as if they were old photographs. Like the one where, as a very young and very tiny little girl in the schoolyard, I am whirling around at arm's length a huge, gigantic gentleman in a suit and tie who is almost the size of our school and who is begging me from high up in the sky: "Have mercy! I promise I won't do it again. Let me down." That was the tax collector of my childhood days. I had never seen him, but I'd heard he was tyrannizing my parents and all the grown-ups I knew.

Childhood memories yellowed by maturity. I keep them in my picture chest. Sometimes I take one out. Just for the fun of it. But the others, the real ones, those that have stood the test of time and stayed with me all these years — these I nurture, cultivate, pursue until my head spins. Just to bring joy to my life.

The most wonderful of all my fantasies is the one where I relinquish my claim to the throne. It isn't so much my being a princess that impresses me in that dream, as having renounced the crown. What thrills me more than anything else is the thought that I am the only one who knows that Prince

Charles is a mere puppet chosen by Queen Elizabeth, my mother, and that if I suddenly felt like it, I could get back my rights to the throne just like that. All I would need to do is go to Buckingham Palace and request an audience.

I thoroughly enjoy playing this part of a princess who returns to the palace in full possession of her rights. I try very hard to bring the same restrained emotion to it each time, the same delicacy of feeling. It is a scene that never ceases to delight me: the Queen, my mother, would have had a happy premonition and as soon as the court usher announces to her that a girl, or a young woman, or a slightly older woman (I've been touching up this tableau for many years now), modestly dressed but noble-minded (he would have seen this in my eyes) is requesting to be received by Her Majesty, she leaves the audience hall and walks towards me, without a crown, or a hat, without anything on her head, in a simple little combed-silk dress — her step is so familiar to me that I have the feeling she is in her dressing gown and slippers. She stops in front of me. Everyone has noticed how close we are standing to each other: one whole pace less than protocol demands. And she says in a voice that is carried by a marble echo to the very back of the vast antechamber:

"My dear child, we are so happy — (no, that's too common, too informal) — we are very pleased that the Empire now has the legitimate heir to the throne back again."

When I have reached this point in my fantasy, I am not quite sure what to do, because I don't want to return to the castle. The official ceremonies, the protocol, one's public image, the distance royalty has to keep, and those hordes of menials watching us constantly, spying on us, turning us into prisoners — I've known it all too well. The life I lead is one I have chosen for myself. It is a humble, modest one, a happy medium as my adoptive mother, my real everyday mother, always says.

So I steer my dream in a different direction. I haven't come to the palace to assert my rights to the throne but to ask the Queen, my mother, for a favour for someone else. That's much more in keeping with who I really am.

What is so good about it, is that I can grow old with this daydream. I was a teenager when I found out that Prince Charles and I were exactly the same age. We had just got television. My mother (my real, everyday mother, not my mother the Queen) and I were glued to the set. We devoured everything it offered us: family sagas, the news, late-night movies, quiz programmes, and even wrestling, bowling, and, I still can't get over it, Sunday Mass, which we would watch when we got home from church.

Consequently, we didn't miss a single one of the images television presented to us when Queen Elizabeth celebrated the tenth anniversary of her reign. For a week she was shown at Buckingham Palace, at the Palace of Westminster, getting on the plane that would take her to Australia, getting off the plane at New Delhi, her blue-, pink-, or yellow-gloved hand, depending on the colour of her outfits, always regally waving, and because she had a very strong sense of family, she would be shown with her children on the palace grounds and in the nursery in a series of strictly official family groupings. The little princes and princess delighted my mother the most.

She is the one who pointed it out to me:

"Did you notice, my darling, that Prince Charles was born the same day you were?"

The coincidence hadn't struck me, but the dreamy smile that lingered on my mother's lips until the end of the programme made me aware that it was an honour to share the date of one's birth with a prince.

The honour was reflected on my mother, since she, too, had something in common with royalty. All evening long she kept telling me the story of my birth, with one detail leading to another, travelling back in time to the beginning: the moment she went through the hospital doors with her scuffed little suitcase which she had touched up with black shoe polish. Entranced, I listened, I asked questions — my birth was taking on a historic dimension and there was a marvellous dream-filled space between us. "Now, what was happening in the meantime at the palace?"

At the palace, I was sure, things weren't going the same way as they were in our hospital's tiny delivery room. The images were superimposed on one another in my mind, they were still quite blurred, yet convincing enough to beguile me. And while my mother carried on with her story, zeroing in on some triviality she had forgotten to mention, my imagery grew clearer, it came alive.

At the palace, the Queen was biting deeply into her lip. Humiliated, mortified, flushed with shame and writhing in pain, her privacy invaded by all those royal officials (I don't know what they are called — chamberlains, Lords, knights — there were about a dozen of them, men, just men, except for two nurses; they have had the mandate to witness the birth of the heir for centuries, I loathed them), she wasn't allowed to moan, she had to deliver the prince without giving a single cry. And although modesty prevented me from looking at the appropriate spot, the sticky little creature covered with mucus and blood that the doctor pulled out from between Her Majesty's legs, happened to be a boy, it was Prince Charles.

It wasn't me, the fantasy hadn't taken shape yet. I was born in a tiny room that smelled of ether, cement dust, and women's discharges. I'm almost tempted to think "in a stable" to make the contrast stand out even more. The delivery taking place in that small room was difficult, painful, because at the last moment I turned head over heels, presented badly, and they had to use forceps to drag me from my mother. "You didn't want to leave me."

She is right, I have never wanted to leave her, not even in my most captivating daydreams.

Ever since the evening we watched that television programme, whenever people asked me how old I was and I answered fourteen, or fifteen, or sixteen, my mother would hurriedly add, "The same age as Prince Charles." And I, delighted and honoured, would stifle my feelings so as not to show how important I felt.

Later on, I found out that the Queen was only a princess when she gave birth to her first child. I didn't concern myself with that detail, the fantasy had already taken shape. Neither did I bother to try and find out when and how I had abandoned Buckingham Palace. I was a princess, that was more than enough. A princess by birth but a commoner by choice, a situation I concealed with a great deal of modesty and pride, and which perfectly suited my wish to live just like everyone else when I knew full well that we had nothing in common.

This is my most dependable daydream. It has never let me down. I have whiled away many wonderful hours with it and still do.

I particularly enjoy imagining that over there at Buckingham Palace all kinds of plots are being hatched to bring me

back into the royal fold. Due to palace wars, or some loathsome sickness, or a scandal rocking the Empire, the whole
Windsor lineage is in danger. And while at the Council of
Ministers they are frantically trying to save the Crown, the
Queen summons the head of the secret service to her state
apartment. Surrounded by richly sculpted panelling, delicately
curved furniture, purple and ermine magnificently displayed
in the portrait gallery, the Queen majestically lowers her voice
when the moment approaches that I relish so much, the one
where she explains I have a birthmark on my right shoulder.

The man stands in front of the Queen, who is standing
herself as she receives him. She says, "A birthmark, in the
shape of a bird poised for flight," and that makes me smile
because I know I do have that mark even though I've only
seen the tip of its tail since the bird's body stretches towards
my shoulder blade. "Bend your head forward a little bit, my
darling, the bird is going to take flight and get caught in your
hair," my mother used to say when she bathed me and
dreamed up games so I wouldn't become restless. It makes me
smile because the man, the one I sometimes call Lord Chamberlain, will be completely fooled once he starts chasing after
me. I never wear sleeveless outfits on the street.

I have fun trying to pick him out among the strangers I
see walking around in our town. Travelling salesmen, inspec-
tors, businessmen in pursuit of something — men dressed as

if they were living out of a suitcase but always freshly shaven and smelling of eau de Cologne, who check the street numbers of houses and stores as they move along. I am especially interested in the ones wearing dark overcoats and soft felt hats. They meet all the requirements. The clothes, their wavering way of walking, the deceptively vacant look in their eyes: they have all the characteristics of a spy who is trying to blend in with the crowd while searching for his prey.

I always jump, I can't help it, when one of them stops me on the street to ask for some information. What if I weren't just making it all up and he really wanted to take me back to Buckingham Palace?

There is one I am particularly afraid of. He wears a charcoal grey overcoat with a matching hat and looks like someone who hasn't got anything to do other than walk around and window-shop, he is exactly like the others, but no eau de Cologne, rather a smell of straw, it seems to me, mixed with the stale odour of old pipe tobacco (he told me he bred dogs, that might explain it, it would make sense) with an extremely gracious manner and a kind expression in his eyes. He returns periodically, once or twice a year, and always finds some excuse to speak to me. I have made quite a few assumptions about him.

The first time he addressed me was a very long time ago.

I had just got a teaching position at Christ-Roi School. I'd rented an apartment halfway between the school and my mother's house, so I only had to go a little bit out of my way along the main street, after my last class of the day, to bring her the things she needed. I remember being very nervous on account of all those new habits which wouldn't settle into a regular pattern yet. Sometimes I say to myself it was simply nervousness, nothing else, and the encounter never really took place.

The first time, then, was on the main street. I was going to the drugstore for my mother and he came walking towards me. The moment I saw him I knew he was going to approach me. He had a shy, weary smile but a very confident look in his eyes, as if we were old acquaintances and he was certain I would do him the favour of recognizing him. So certain that, as he came nearer, his smile became broader and broader. Once he reached me, he positively beamed.

"Hello," he said, looking straight into my eyes.

He had taken his hat off as if he wanted to make it easier for me to recognize him, and I could see a tuft of pale-yellowish hair standing up on a balding head. I didn't even try to take a closer look at him — his eyes, his nose, his mouth, if he was handsome, young, or old — because his voice had thrown me into a terrible panic. It was a gentle, vulnerable voice, with something painfully familiar about it. So I wouldn't have to listen to it any more, I hurriedly got to the point.

"Are you looking for something?"

"No, I'm looking for somebody." His smile was almost ecstatic.

That was going too far. The fantasy was catching up with me in real life. I suddenly felt scared, and dashed into the nearest store, a boutique selling fine lingerie. I must have spent at least an hour fingering the silk and lace undergarments the saleswoman showed me while I kept an eye on the street to make sure Lord Chamberlain had well and truly disappeared. I finally chose a flannel dressing gown. To please the saleswoman, but especially to have an excuse to give my mother for being so late.

By then, my mother wasn't going out any more. I had become her only contact with the outside world, and still am. My late-afternoon visits make it possible for her to stay on course. I tell her about everything. How I snagged my stocking on something in the morning, how the principal greeted me in a more friendly way than usual, about my students, the mischief they get into and also their accomplishments, what happened at the playground, about my lunch with my colleagues and the stories they share with me, the people I run into on the street, especially if they are people she knows, and on and on it goes like this for hours on end.

We always have a good time because we both enjoy making fun of people. All it takes is some speech defect, or a shaky marital situation (which is more and more common nowadays), or someone's unusual hairiness, or a poorly kept secret — the people involved are guaranteed to have a pretty nasty time of it from us.

I didn't mean to say a word to her about that man I met on the street. On my way back, I'd convinced myself there had been no Lord Chamberlain. Luckily, my foray into the boutique provided us with more than enough to talk about. Neither of us had been in there before, we always shopped for our underwear in department stores, and it was inconceivable to us that women might be wearing such an orgy of lace underneath their clothes and especially that they might be paying those prices.

"And you were there for a whole hour?" my mother asked, astonished.

I simply had to tell her.

She was interested in what the stranger wore, the way he approached me, the way he walked and talked — she went back over certain details, "A smell of old pipe tobacco?" quizzing me about things that hadn't struck me. "Did he look neat? No stains on his coat?" and concluded by saying, "You did the right thing. Men who approach women on the street aren't dangerous as long as one ignores them."

This conversation reassured me. The stranger had become a stranger again. He had returned to the anonymity of being just another old gentleman in an overcoat. Because of that, I felt bold enough, when I got home in the early evening, to relive my fear of Lord Chamberlain simply for the fun of it. What if he wanted to... yes, what if he'd really wanted to take me back to Buckingham Palace? The fear I felt was deliciously frightening. So I decided that, if that man ever turned up again, I would only confront him in my daydreams.

A wise decision because, of course, he turned up again and I didn't find it hard at all any more to snub him. As the years went by, the overcoat changed, as did the hat — from charcoal grey they went to brown, to taupe, then back to charcoal grey. The man got old, he only has a thin ring of hair left now. His smile has dimmed. From old age, or from always seeing me act as if I didn't know him. He is getting old before his time, he is hurrying towards his old age, as my mother says.

He gave up following me on the street a long time ago. He had become a pitiful sight. With his hair turned white, stooped, worn-out, with the jerky gait of an arthritic, he never got a chance to speak to me, because the moment he started to say something, I would dash away.

I now see him in the park.

Sometimes in the evening before dusk, when the sun grows weary and leaves only a soft golden trail, or on weekend afternoons, between cleaning my apartment and preparing for school, I take a rest, and while I sit at a bench, preferably deep inside a cluster of evergreens, which I enjoy for their smell and their shade, I will slip into my other life. And, looking out over the river which flows through the grassy dells of the park between two steep cliffs and could easily be Shakespeare's Thames if it weren't so clear and so wild, I practise being a royal. I will sit up very straight, place both my hands flat on my right thigh, with one hand resting on top of the other, and tuck my legs back a little bit beneath the bench. This is how I like to see myself. Just like the Queen Mother in a photograph from the time of King George VI. The Queen Mother, may God forgive me, has always seemed haughtier to me than my mother the Queen. In that particular photo the King looks like the rose grower he really is and the Princesses Elizabeth and Margaret resemble well-behaved little country girls. It is the Queen Mother who looks truly regal because of her smile, her bearing, and her gaze.

I will choose some theme, any theme will do — the Queen visiting our town as part of a royal tour, the principal finding out I am heir to the English throne — and I will keep myself happily occupied for hours.

Quite often I haven't seen him coming and I'll suddenly notice him sitting on my right, the side of my birthmark which is poised for flight.

He will speak to me. And it's always a shock to hear that gentle, familiar voice. He is embarrassingly humble. He tells me things I am unable to fit into my fantasies. Like that business about dog breeding he keeps talking about.

"We've tried to crossbreed a Laika bitch with a Husky, but it didn't work out. Yet the bitch is fertile. She has had three litters with a Samoyed. The Husky, too, has bred without any difficulty. We're beginning to think the two breeds are incompatible. The vet disagrees. He says we're picking the wrong time. Yet it seems to me..."

Dog breeding, that's what he does for a living, apparently.

"There isn't much money in it. What with the cost of the dog food and the vet — when we manage to sell a dog, there isn't much left over at the end of the month. Even so, I've never failed to send a money order. I've never..."

He always leaves silences. He will be waiting for me to jump in, to reveal myself. But I won't say a word, I'll just keep very still. What if people saw me sitting here on my bench talking to myself? I am already having to deal with a group of insolent young people. They hang around the park at all hours and I have often overheard them making unkind remarks about me. So I hold the pose and think to myself that the dream will go away.

Actually, I have no trouble getting rid of it. The moment I want it to stop, I simply get up and leave. He never follows me.

Sometimes a whole year goes by before the man shows up again. I have lots of time then to imagine all sorts of things about him.

I tell myself he really exists, that he hasn't got anything to do with my daydreams. He is an eccentric, a mad vagabond who adopts people as he passes through a town and casts them in imaginary parts in his life. Or he could be a sentimental old man, a Casanova past his prime who is chancing another conquest. He might also be, as my mother recently said to me, some melancholy old man who keeps turning up and vanishing again so that he can entrench himself in our lives. "Don't let him do it."

But when I haven't seen him in a long time, I find myself searching for him among all those strangers wearing overcoats. Then he will suddenly be there, by my side, like an old acquaintance.

Well, really, a dog breeder... Surely, they could have thought of something better, couldn't they? It isn't a suitable position for someone of Lord Chamberlain's station. I suppose they felt I would let myself be taken in more easily if they sent someone who had a modest background. For the same reason, they must have carried out an investigation into the life I lead over here. The man has some very accurate information about my childhood, my mother, my father.

"The house is still in pretty good shape. I'm really pleased about that, there isn't one shingle missing from the roof. But it would be a good idea to have the siding redone. One made of vinyl would be best. Tell your mother to check underneath the asphalt-shingle siding, there might be some patches of rotten wood. She ought to get somebody to inspect the boards below the bathroom window — if there's one spot where moisture might have got in, that's where it would be. Vinyl shouldn't be too expensive. Tell her not to worry about the cost, my dear. I'll contribute a little more if necessary."

To be spoken to in such a familiar way is something I've never been able to get used to. Only at school and with women either I or my mother have been friends with for a long time does it seem perfectly natural, even though with my students I still find it difficult to accept these new educational methods which allow them to talk to me a if we were close friends. I feel I have reached an age that imposes a certain distance.

When a stranger talks to me like that, it is improper, simply unacceptable. I wish I could be certain this man really exists, that he isn't just a figment of my imagination, but a creature of flesh and blood and human intelligence. I would be sure to give him of a piece of my mind. I would tell him he has no right to sit on my bench and talk to me as if he knew me intimately. But, above all, I would tell him to stop talking to me about my mother.

"She is such an unusual woman. She is really a child at heart. One should never be abrupt with her. A cross word, an angry look, or some trivial little thing — and her world can shatter into a thousand pieces. She is terribly fragile. You should just humour her. When it's absolutely necessary, but only when it is necessary, try to make your point very slowly, very gradually, so she won't even be aware of it. Otherwise, simply let her look at things in her own way. That's when she is at her best — a lovely little jewel nestled in its felt box."

Since my mother stopped going out, people have been tactful enough not to talk to me about her, or else so briefly or in such a conventional way that I only need to reply: "Yes, she's fine, thank you; I'll give her your regards." Yet he would like me to tell him if she is aging gracefully, if she still wears her hair long, if it's completely white or has a blue rinse in it, if she still looks out the window in the morning greeting the birds with a song — as though he had known her all his life.

The last time, he went on about his dog breeding again. He tacked on a story about an earthy, no-nonsense woman.

A woman who took him in when he was in a very bad way, who didn't ask him for anything but gave him everything. She isn't pretty like my mother. She isn't subtle or precious like her. *Precious*, that's what he said. She's as rough as the bark of a pine tree, a hard worker with a zest for life who has both feet firmly planted on the ground. She breeds dogs; he does his best to help her, and for the most part he is contented.

I decided that was the end of Lord Chamberlain. None of it made any sense any more. Prince Charles, my mother the Queen, my real mother, the stranger in his old overcoat, the dog breeding, all those conversations on the park bench, the fear, the waiting, the fear, and now that woman — it just didn't hold together any more. At the cost of my daydreams, at the cost of reality which I would now have to experience head-on, I had to put an end to it.

I got up and walked all the way to the fence-like barrier the town has put up along the steep slope of the riverbank. I waited. I waited for the shadowy figure to catch up with me. He came. We trudged along the fence line. I could hear him panting behind me. I led him to one of those sections of the fence that are regularly vandalized by young delinquents so they can slip through to the side where the public isn't allowed and listen to the splash their stones make when they toss them into the river.

I stepped through the opening where the slats of the fence

had been knocked down and then strolled along the edge of the cliff as leisurely as someone who is enjoying the scenery. The shadowy figure kept following me. He was beginning to gasp for breath. When I reached the cliff's highest point, I made my move. I swivelled around and saw the happy look in his eyes. He took a step towards me, stretched out his arms, for a kiss, a hug. I only had to give a pull on his right arm, the arm nearest to the river, and the stranger's body followed, it toppled over the edge.

I looked around. There was no one there. I'm the only one to know and not to know what happened.

That wasn't long ago. It's still too soon to tell if the fantasy will return, if Lord Chamberlain will suddenly re-emerge from my daydreams.

I'm a little worried about the life that lies ahead of me. No grandiose dreams on the horizon, no exciting fear to keep me on the alert — I'll need to cultivate the other ones, the one with Robin Hood and all my other daydreams, I'll have to give them a new dimension.

That dream of being a princess in a faraway land was too heavy a burden. I had to give it up once and for all. I did what I had to do. And yet...

And yet I wonder how the Queen would react if a royal tour brought her to our little town one day and I was presented to her.

I think my father has died. A month ago, perhaps two. No longer than that. My mother couldn't possibly manage without a money order any longer than that.

It's not the fact of having to support both my mother and myself on my salary that worries me. There are women among my colleagues who provide for families with two, three, or even four children solely on what they earn from teaching. No, what worries me is how to preserve her dignity. Already she has found it difficult to let me know about her straitened circumstances.

The first time, I thought it was simply an oversight. I had brought her the groceries. Normally she makes a little list for me the day before and I bring her her things the next day after school. She always asks me in a nice way: "Would you mind getting something for me at the drugstore?" or "I haven't got time to go to the bank, could you..." as if she still needed to ask, when this has been part of our regular routine for the last twenty years — ever since she gave up going out. I arrive at the house, unpack the bag, "That's sweet of you, you didn't forget," put the things away and leave the tape from the cash register on the kitchen counter. Then we chat. We always enjoy ourselves, while I'm getting our meal ready and when we sit down to eat and, later, while I'm washing the dishes. We make fun of people's shortcomings and life's peculiarities. It's as light as a bubble and as pointed as the needle that's about to puncture it, it's a wonderful part of our day. Before I leave, I will always find the exact amount on the counter.

That time, though, there was no money, only the tape from the cash register. I assumed, "She has forgotten." The next day there was nothing, neither tape nor money. Don't give it a thought, I said to myself, forget about it. I didn't want to upset her by acting in a way that wasn't quite natural.

Over the next few days, the register tapes became painfully conspicuous by their absence. Yet, in my utter stupidity, I never asked myself what this absence might mean. All I could think of was I mustn't upset our habits, that I mustn't sound the alarm. I was torn between what to do and what not to do. Walk over to the counter and pretend to pick up the money that wasn't there, play the part of someone who simply forgets to go over to the counter on her way out, keep putting the register tape on the counter, or stop putting it there. And all this time my dear mother was waiting for me to finally grasp her predicament.

It took a great deal of recklessness on her part to decide on the ultimate gesture, the one that would make our new circumstances perfectly clear to both of us. What she did, and the sheer cleverness of her gesture still amazes me, is put the return envelope of her hydro bill in a prominent position on the counter. The message was unmistakable. The envelope had the bill in it but no cheque. She was asking me to pay her hydro bill.

That was Thursday, yesterday, the day I do her grocery shopping. As soon as I opened the envelope, I realized I would also have to pay the gas bill, the water bill, her taxes, her insurance premiums — she no longer had any means of support, there were no money orders any more. And to show that this was all right with me, I slipped the envelope as well as the cash-register tape for the groceries into my coat pocket.

Our conversation was particularly airy. Each of us made sure it didn't get stuck on anything that might be too weighty. All this manoeuvring exhausted me, and it wasn't until later that evening, after I got back to my apartment, that I stopped to think about there not being any money orders.

It has been quite a while since I have thought about my father and I find it difficult to form an image of him in my mind. I have to refer to his photograph on the living-room wall at my mother's house in order to remember what he was like. His shy, almost self-effacing smile, his iridescent blue eyes, and his thin blond hair which made him look boyish even though he was beginning to go bald; my girlfriends thought he was handsome. As for the rest — his long, lithe body, the restrained way in which he moved, always held back by an excessively gentle side to his nature, and his voice, his deep, melodious voice — I have to make an effort before it all comes back to me. So many years have gone by that I've almost forgotten.

I wonder if my mother will put a black band on my father's photograph and if she is going to give herself permission to go into mourning now that she knows that I know. I don't suppose so. We did our grieving a long time ago.

Perhaps she will finally agree to go out. I have always felt that he was partly responsible, that she lived like a recluse in the house because of him. Actually, I think he came back once. But the evidence is so slim... A smell of tobacco, that same smell of pipe tobacco she used to fight against with her arsenal of disinfectants and deodorizers while the three of us still lived together, which I detected immediately when I got home.

I was in my final year. I was just about to get my teaching certificate. That prospect excited her enormously and, since it was exam time, I would no sooner step into the hallway than she would bombard me with questions about the exam I had just taken and the one that was coming up next.

That afternoon, I found her slumped in an armchair, the

chair that had been my father's, which we now reserved for visitors. There was no meal being prepared, my mother was in an almost catatonic state, she didn't speak, didn't stir, just barely blinked, and there was that strong smell of tobacco lingering in the room. Right away my intuition told me what had happened.

She remained huddled in the armchair for several days. Dr. Marsan came, but there was nothing he could do. She wouldn't let him listen to her heartbeat, refused to take any medication and, naturally, refused to be hospitalized. I looked after everything — the meals, the housework, the shopping — while at the same time cramming for my exams. The results I got weren't nearly as good as my general average.

Little by little, her vitality returned. After a week of bowls of chicken broth, of custard puddings, hot-water bottles, and compresses, she abandoned the armchair and quietly began running the house again. She was still too weak to go out, though, and that is why I continued to do the shopping.

I don't know if I was actually expecting an explanation. For a very long time we had been used to tackling important matters only by hinting at them or by meaningful glances. Insisting on an explanation showed a lack of consideration for the feelings it might arouse.

All she said about it was: "A love that is deep and true is wedded to eternity, not to this life."

A remark I meticulously decoded and which revealed to me the profound love she continued to feel for my father, the hope she cherished for the next world, and perhaps her weariness in the face of the long stretch of life still ahead of her — a remark which gave me no indication, however, as to what to think of the tobacco smoke.

Then later, a few weeks later, she added, "Love has the flawless beauty of a diamond, it can't be patched up like an old sheet."

And I realized she meant the love that causes pain, that breaks your heart, the kind of love they sing about in sad, romantic love songs. She had closed her door to him and was afraid of meeting him on the street. She wanted her love to remain unchanged, exactly like it was when she lived with him. He was offering her some kind of compromise, but she wanted the flawless beauty of a diamond. Poor dear little Mama! She mustn't see him again, it would be the end of her. I had no difficulty getting used to doing what the situation demanded. Although she was now completely well again and had resumed her war against microbes and dust, and there was no trace of her turmoil left, she continued to ask me, "Would you mind going to… " and I would go to the drugstore, to the bank, get her groceries — I was happy to do her shopping, it seemed as if it was the most natural thing in the world.

She was forty-five years old. I was twenty. The structure

of our lives had reached a turning point at the precise moment when we chose to erase the smell of tobacco from our memory. She has shut herself up in the house while I am active in the outside world: with my work, at my apartment, going into town to shop, doing a little bit of house cleaning for her on Saturdays, socializing with our old acquaintances whom I have gradually taught to ask me only the most general questions about my mother. We lead a comfortable, well-ordered life.

She is the one who got me to move into an apartment. It had never entered my mind that we might have to part some day.

I had received my certificate and was waiting for my first job. It was easy to find employment at the time and I was sure I would have a teaching position in September. So I felt very confident and calm as I embarked on my first school vacation as an adult. With the previous month's turmoil duly forgotten, we were now cosily settled in our new routine. Only the women in our neighbourhood and the women who were friends of ours made us feel somewhat uncomfortable by showing surprise and asking seemingly innocent questions.

At first I didn't take any notice of it, but, as the summer wore on, various household items were added to the shopping list. Sheets, towels, pots and pans, other kitchen utensils and I don't know what else, things I didn't see any need for since my mother had a good supply of all that. When she began to include appliances, I reacted. I let the kettle go by, as well as an iron and a blender, but when she asked for a vacuum cleaner, I couldn't help voicing the question that had been looming in my eyes.

"Well, you need a trousseau, don't you?"

A trousseau, to my mind, meant marriage, and I had absolutely no plans in that direction. I began to stammer out a denial but she was already forging ahead, I had to hear her out.

"Listen, my darling. You're all grown up now. You have finished your studies, you have a fine profession, I'm proud of you. This is the beginning of a new life for you, your life as an adult, and you've got to do things properly. For a start, you must find yourself a nice little apartment. An independent young lady doesn't live with her parents. What would people say? That I'm totally useless? That I can't look after myself?"

When my mother put it that way, I had no choice but to go along with her wishes.

And I moved into the apartment where I still live today — where I have been brooding since yesterday. I've always had trouble sleeping, but last night I barely slept at all. I added up all our expenses. We will manage very well on my salary. We would even be able to travel. I doubt she'll agree to leave the house, however.

But how will I be able to pay for absolutely everything — her gas bills, her clothes, her magazines, her knitting wool, her fragrances, her denture-cleansers — without undermining her dignity? How am I going to deal with buying presents for myself at Christmas and for my birthday? I have examined this question from every angle but haven't found anything that might help me to give, and help her to receive, without creating that dreadful feeling of indebtedness that would damage our relationship and humiliate us, myself just as much as her, since I could never tolerate seeing her mortified by gratitude.

I cherish the hope that she may have been thinking about this predicament much longer than I have. She probably focussed on it as soon as the money order was seriously overdue. She may already have devised a solution, a way of handling it that will save us both from humiliation.

I also remind myself that as far as thorny predicaments are concerned, we have experienced worse ones. What I have in mind here is... I'm afraid to say the word, I find it simply too revolting when I have to apply it to my own mother.

It's Dr. Marsan who came out with it.

I was relieved to hear a few years ago that he had died. I could finally switch to another doctor. We now see Dr. Sulong, who is held in contempt by everyone in town because he is Asian but who is willing to make house calls and doesn't know anything about our family history. My annual check-up with Dr. Marsan used to be an ordeal I put off from one month to the next. He had a way of conducting the gynecological examination that I found unbearable. "We still have our little hymen then, do we? Perhaps you'll be luckier next year." And at the end of the consultation, after giving me a clean bill of health, he would ask after my mother and even after my father. That really was the last straw. "Still no news? That's too bad. He was a good man, an awfully patient man."

Just because he knew our bodies, he felt he could search our souls. I was especially afraid of him that day when my yearly check-up took place a couple of months after the tobacco-smell upheaval. I was terrified he would ask more specific questions about my father.

After weighing me, listening to my chest, checking my throat and reflexes, and once the loathsome gynecological examination was over, he settled down at his desk to prescribe a tonic for me. The recent turmoil had left me with a vitamin deficiency.

"As for your mother, her incontinence problem..."

I almost shot up from my chair. I had been well aware for some time of certain changes at the house. There was the laundry, which my mother was now doing every day, a huge laundry that filled up the entire clothesline, with everything from her bed hanging out there: the sheets, the blankets, the pillow cases, and even her pink chenille bedspread. Also, she now wore a clean dress every day. Then there was that really strong perfume, Ciel de Paris, which my father had given her ages ago and she had always refused to wear ("I feel like a tart when I've put it on"), the scent of which now hung heavily in every part of the house without totally covering up, however, that other, lingering, slightly acid smell that I didn't want to investigate.

"... there's nothing we can do, it's caused by nerves. She has had a shock, a severe emotional shock. Do you have any idea what that could be? I've suggested a catheter to her but, you know her, she wouldn't hear of it."

Even after the tobacco smell, after she came out of her torpor and the armchair cushion had needed to be washed thoroughly, I still shut my mind to all questions. Then came those phenomenal quantities of sanitary napkins she put down on her shopping list week after week. I blamed it on her being pre-menopausal. It's a well-known fact: women very nearly break down at that stage of their lives.

What if I had actually asked myself questions and come up with answers... No, I had the good sense not to fall into that trap. My life was a tangled mess in those days. I used to get horrible migraines whenever I tried to sort things out. It is all still a frightening muddle in my mind, my mother's torpor, that inexplicable emotional shock, Dr. Marsan, Lord Chamberlain, that tobacco smell and... my mother's smell.

I resented Dr. Marsan for it. If he hadn't been so blunt, I could have continued to believe she was simply experiencing some pre-menopausal complications. Instead of which I have had to do a lot of skillful manoeuvering all these years so she could remain convinced she had managed to conceal her humiliation from me.

The smell now pervades the house in such a way that, in spite of all those loads of laundry and our huge collection of chemicals, I am occasionally bothered by it. Especially in the cold of winter, when we can't leave any windows open. I will use anything as an excuse then for scrubbing the house from top to bottom. But that lingering, vinagery smell of cheap stale old wine never goes away. There are times when I have the impression I am carrying it along with me to my apartment and to school like a long trail of decaying life. I feel nostalgia for my mother's menstruation smell.

Sanitary napkins haven't been sufficient for quite a while. The problem has become more extensive over the years. Dr. Marsan briefly commented on it during my last visit to his office. That was five years ago. He died a few months later. He said something about a disposable undergarment.

"It's the best thing available right now. You can get them with or without elastic straps, with or without a waistband. They come in various sizes. They're disposable, like diapers."

"Like diapers," as if, just like that, I could bring my mother diapers for adults. As if I could do such a thing without her having asked me for them first. "Like diapers." That explanation didn't make any sense at all.

I did take a look at those undergarments. Actually, whenever I'm walking through the drugstore's aisle of feminine-hygiene products, I keep on going until I reach the disposable underwear, just in case I discover some new aspect of them, some new approach that would make it possible for me to bring them to my mother. It really is what I'm looking for. But how to go about it?

Tomorrow is Saturday, my day for doing a little bit of housework at my mother's place. On Sunday we listen to the symphony orchestra concert on the radio. Two days of sheer contentment which we'll spend studiously avoiding the subject of the absent money orders. Yet during all this time my father will be with us — his photograph, his memory, his death. We will have to skirt around our thoughts, face each other with expressionless eyes, twist our way between her consciousness and mine, so that the only reality left will be the two of us and how happy we are together.

I wonder how long will it be before he really dies. We worked so hard at keeping him dead while he was still alive that his memory, now that we have to believe he is dead, is clinging to life more than ever.

I wonder, too, what motive they would ascribe to me if one day I happened to be accused of killing him.